My

Sound Box

by Jane Belk Moncure

illustrated by Linda Sommers

THE CHILD'S WORLD

ELGIN, ILLINOIS 60120

Distributed by Childrens Press, 1224 West Van Buren Street,
Chicago, Illinois 60607.

Library of Congress Cataloging in Publication Data

Moncure, Jane Belk.
  My t sound box.

  (Sound box books)
  SUMMARY: A little boy fills his sound box with many
words beginning with the letter "t".
  [1. Alphabet books] I. Sommers, Linda.
II. Title. III. Series.
PZ7.M739Myt   [E]   77-23587
ISBN 0-913778-96-6

My "t" Sound Box

(Blends are included in this book.)

Little  had a

"I will find things that begin with my "t" sound," he said.

"I will put them into my sound  box.

I like toys. I will
look for toys."

Little  found a toy train

on a
train track.

Did he put the toy train and the
track into his box? He did!

Little  found a toy

Did he put the tractor into the box with the toy train and the track?

He did!

Then Little  found a truck.

He drove that truck up,   up,

10

up a tall mountain.

He drove to the top,
the very tip-top!

At the top of the tall mountain, he found two turtles.

Did he put the two turtles into his box?

He did!

box

Then he found a  toad.

Did he put the toad into the box?

He did!

Now the box was so full that he could not see over the top.
He tripped!
He tumbled

down,

down,

down

the mountain.
He tumbled into a turkey.

Turkey feathers flew!

So Little  made a turkey-feather hat.

He and the turkey danced together.

Little  found a tom-tom.

He tapped the tom-tom,
"Tom, tum, tum!
Tom, tum, tum!"

Then he found a tomahawk.

Little  and the turkey

danced some more.

Then he put the turkey,
the tom-tom, and the
tomahawk into his box.

Suddenly Little  heard a terrific noise!

box

He ran

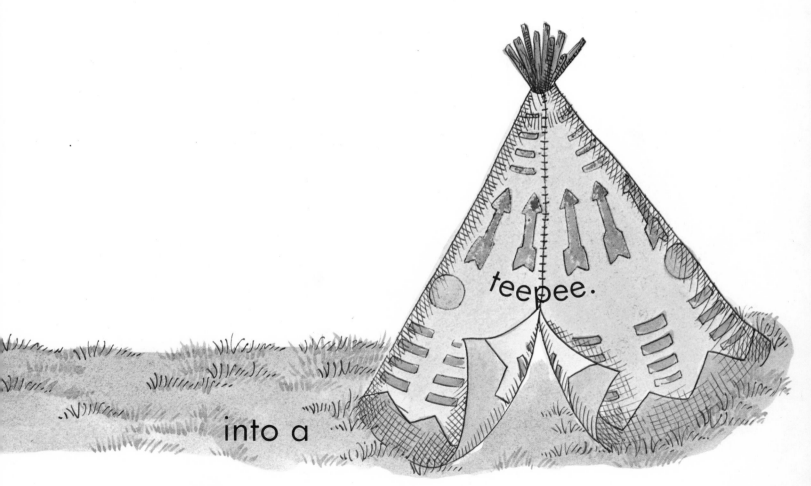

into a   teepee.

When he looked out, he saw a

tiger.

The tiger opened his mouth. There were many

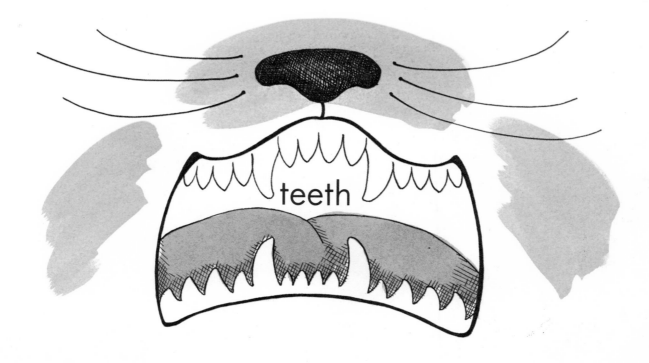

teeth

in the tiger's mouth!

"I have a loose tooth," said the tiger.
"Please pull out my tooth!"

So Little   pulled out the tooth.

Then Little  and the tiger went inside the teepee. They played with all the toys in the box.

tiger

two turtles

toad

truck

tom-tom

train track

omahawk

train

turkey

tractor

They had a terrific time!

27

Can you read these words with Little ?

telephone

tulip

tray

tricycle

toe

tree

28

tomato

toothbrush

television

tie

table

top

taco

tire

teapot

29

About the Author

Jane Belk Moncure, author of many books and stories for young children, is a graduate of Virginia Commonwealth University and Columbia University. She has taught nursery, kindergarten and primary children in Europe and America. Mrs. Moncure has taught early childhood education while serving on the faculties of Virginia Commonwealth University and the University of Richmond. She was the first president of the Virginia Association for Early Childhood Education and has been recognized widely for her services to young children. She is married to Dr. James A. Moncure, Vice President of Elon College, and currently teaches in Burlington, North Carolina.